EDDIE
and the
Spiders

Carpenter Aunt

Eddie and the Spiders

iUniverse books may be ordered through booksellers or by contacting:

iUniverse
1663 Liberty Drive
Bloomington, IN 47403
www.iuniverse.com
844-349-9409

Because of the dynamic nature of the Internet, any web addresses or links contained in this book may have changed since publication and may no longer be valid. The views expressed in this work are solely those of the author and do not necessarily reflect the views of the publisher, and the publisher hereby disclaims any responsibility for them.

Any people depicted in stock imagery provided by Getty Images are models, and such images are being used for illustrative purposes only. Certain stock imagery © Getty Images.

ISBN: 978-1-6632-6699-6 (sc)
978-1-6632-6700-9 (e)

Library of Congress Control Number: 2024919841

Print information available on the last page.

iUniverse rev. date: 09/17/2024

Eddieduction

Eddie is a teddy bear originally from South Dakota, who now lives in Southern Indiana. He was a gift to me, from my husband on one of his hunting trips.

Hi! I am Eddie the teddy bear. Being a teddy bear is not easy, but it is really fun. I am five years old, live on a cattle farm, am blessed with Autism and I love to explore and learn new things. Autism allows me to view the world differently.

Today I am exploring spiders, in order to learn the different types of spiders and why they scare mom so bad. Mom said that she does not mind if I go spider hunting today, as long as I don't invite them to supper. I promised mom that I wouldn't.

3

I head outside to start my spider hunt. Spiders are everywhere, if you look for them. I head to the garden first and carefully check around. I found one! This one is a garden spider!

I race inside to tell mom that I found a garden spider. Mom asks, "How did you know it was a garden spider?" I tell mom, "A garden spider wears a straw hat and gardening gloves and carries a rake!" Mom said, "I guess I haven't paid much attention to garden spiders lately." I shake my head at mom and run back out the door.

I decide to go down to the creek to spider hunt. In no time I see a brown spider driving a spider size sailboat down the creek. When the spider gets closer, I realize that it is wearing a blue rain coat, red rainboots and is carrying an umbrella. Wow, that must be a water spider!

I hurry back to the house to tell mom about the new spider I saw in the raincoat. Mom asks, "What kind of spider was it?" I said, "A water spider!" Mom said, "Of course. Why didn't I think of that." Mom said that she is starting to get creeped out now due to the spiders and has given me some blank paper and crayons to draw the next spiders I meet, so I won't have to come in and tell her about them. So, back outside I go!

I think I will take a walk through the woods and continue my spider hunt. I heard a small voice holler, "Look out below!" I look up to see a spider jump from a tree to the ground. I look closely at the spider as it lands. It has a little parachute on it's back. Awesome, that is the first jumping spider I have seen! I draw a quick picture, so I don't forget to tell mom at bed time.

I continue my walk through the woods and in no time, I come across another spider dressed in camouflage carrying a net. I sit quietly on a log and watch him. Suddenly he jumps forward and drops his net! He caught a fly! I bet he is a hunting spider! I waste no time with drawing him on my paper and hurry on my way. Afterall, a hunting spider might not only hunt flies, he may hunt teddy bears too.

I walk back up towards the house through the field. On my walk I noticed that my friend Aaron has left the combine in the corn field. I love riding in the combine with him, so I climb inside. To my surprise, there is a spider getting ready to drive this combine to harvest the rest of the corn. "What kind of spider are you," I asked the spider. "I am a corn spider. My job is to help bring in the corn crop in the fall." "Glad to meet you," I said. I drew her picture on my paper and climbed down out of the combine to continue my journey.

I soon hear a little voice crying. I follow the noise to find a spider in the field crying. I notice that she is dressed in black and has a black vial over her face. She explained that a bird just ate her husband and she was now a black widow. I apologized for her misfortune and went on my way.

15

The sun is starting to set, so I better get on home. I am almost home when I hear another small voice asking how I am doing this evening. I reply that I am fine, as I look around. Then I spot this yellow spider next to a tree in the yard. I ask' "What kind of spider are you?" "I am a banana spider" the spider replies. "A banana spider? There are no bananas around here," I tell her. The spider explains to me that she was vacationing here and decided to stay. "Where did you buy your house," I ask? "From the house spider. He sells houses on the web," she tells me. I let the spider know that I am glad to meet her, and I head on in the house.

As I eat supper with my mom and dad, I tell them all about all the different spiders I met today.

I take my bath, then mom tucks me into bed. I hear a little howling noise outside my window. I look out the window to see a full moon in the sky. I listen closely to the howling noise and I trace it to this little spider sitting on the side of the house. I ask mom, "What kind of spider is that?" Mom says, "It is a wolf spider. They howl at the moon." Mom tucks me into bed again and kisses me good night.

I fall asleep quickly. I had a very busy day!

Printed in the United States
by Baker & Taylor Publisher Services